SHORT TALES

NORSE MYTHS

ODIN

Adapted by
Shannon Eric Denton

Illustrated by
Mark Bloodworth

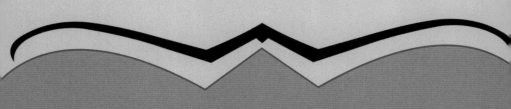

visit us at www.abdopublishing.com

Published by Magic Wagon, a division of the ABDO Publishing Group, 8000 West 78th Street, Edina, Minnesota, 55439. Copyright © 2011 by Abdo Consulting Group, Inc. International copyrights reserved in all countries. All rights reserved. No part of this book may be reproduced in any form without written permission from the publisher.

Short Tales ™ is a trademark and logo of Magic Wagon.

Printed in the United States of America, North Mankato, Minnesota.
032010
092010
This book contains at least 10% recycled materials.

Adapted Text by Shannon Eric Denton
Illustrations by Mark Bloodworth
Colors by Wes Hartman
Edited by Stephanie Hedlund and Rochelle Baltzer
Interior Layout by Kristen Fitzner Denton
Book Design and Packaging by Shannon Eric Denton

Library of Congress Cataloging-in-Publication Data

Denton, Shannon Eric.
  Odin / adapted by Shannon Eric Denton ; illustrated by Mark Bloodworth.
    p. cm. -- (Short tales. Norse myths)
  ISBN 978-1-60270-568-5
  1. Odin (Norse deity)--Juvenile literature. I. Bloodworth, Mark. II. Title.
  BL870.O3D46 2009
  398.209363'01--dc22
                              2008032525

THE NORSE GODS

ODIN:
The All-Father
of the Gods

FRIGGA:
Queen of
the Gods

BALDUR:
The Best Loved
of the Gods

FORSETI:
God of
Justice

HEIMDALL:
The Guardian
of Asgard

HOD:
God of Winter

THOR:
God of Thunder

TYR:
God of War

HERMOD:
Messenger of
the Gods

FREYR:
God of Weather

LOKI:
The Trickster

FREYA:
Goddess of
Beauty and Love

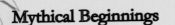

Mythical Beginnings

Life in the universe began with fire and ice. As the heat hit the cold, the giant Ymir and the icy cow Audhumla were created.

Ymir then created the giants. He also created the first man, whom he named Búri. Búri married a giantess, and they had a son named Bor. Bor grew up and had three sons named Odin, Vili, and Ve.

Odin would become the most powerful god due to his immense knowledge. It would help him become the All-Father of the Norse gods.

As teenagers, Odin and his brothers wanted the world for themselves. So, they slew the mighty giant Ymir.

Odin, Vili, and Ve then created seven more worlds. They used Ymir's flesh for dirt, his blood for water, and his bones for stone.

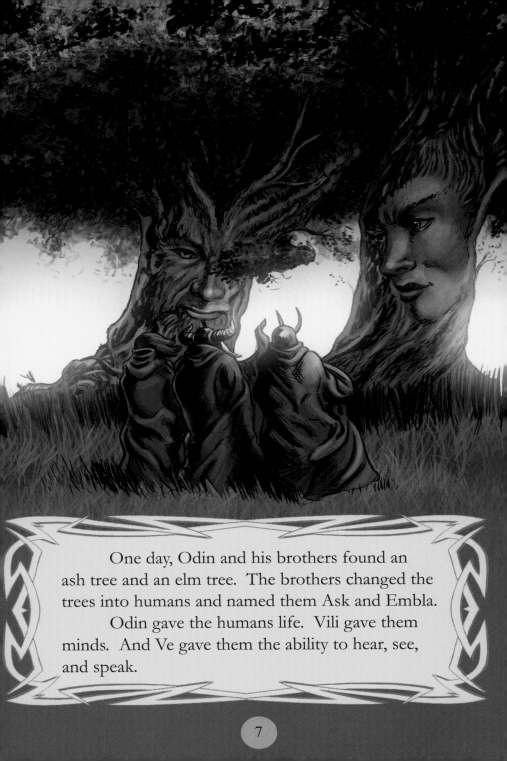

One day, Odin and his brothers found an ash tree and an elm tree. The brothers changed the trees into humans and named them Ask and Embla.

Odin gave the humans life. Vili gave them minds. And Ve gave them the ability to hear, see, and speak.

Odin and his brothers then built the kingdom of Middle Earth for their humans. They placed a huge fence around Middle Earth to keep the giants out.

Ask and Embla were happy in Middle Earth. They fell in love, married, and had children.

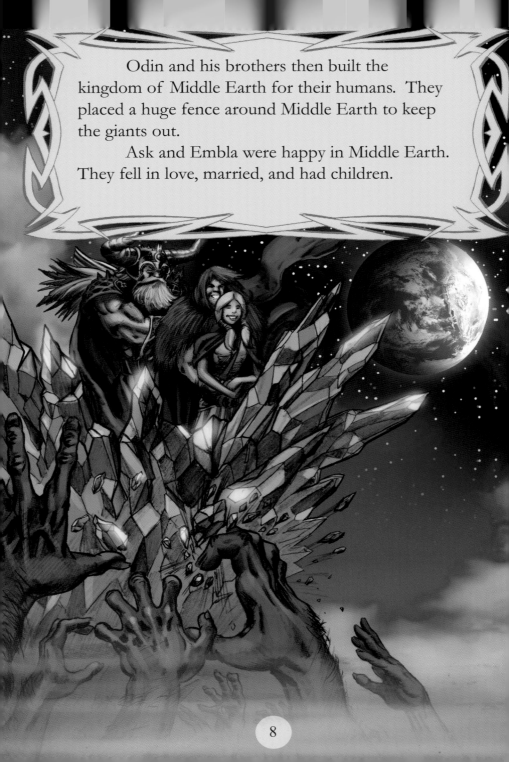

Odin wished to have the kind of happiness Ask and Embla had. Soon, Odin met a woman named Frigga. He fell in love with Frigga and married her.

Odin and Frigga had three sons named Baldur, Hoor, and Thor. Odin loved his sons very much. He decided to build a kingdom worthy of them.

Odin brought his family to Asgard, the capital of the ruling gods. There, he built three halls for his children.

First Odin built Gladsheim, a vast hall where he ruled the twelve Judges. These people oversaw the affairs of Asgard.

Odin then built Valaskjálf, a silver hall with a throne. From the throne, Odin could see the whole earth.

Finally, Odin built Valhalla. It had 540 gates and a large hall containing golden shields, spears, and armor.

As he completed Valhalla, Odin realized his blind son Hoor would never see his creations. Odin set off on a quest to find a way for Hoor to see.

On his quest, Odin journeyed across his many worlds. He was gone for years and had many adventures.

Odin discovered magical items on these journeys. He won a spear called Gungnir, which never misses its target.

He claimed a magical gold ring called Draupnir. Every ninth night, eight new rings sprang from this magic ring.

Odin also made friends with two magical ravens named Thought and Memory. Years after Odin's quest, these ravens would fly around Midgard and report the happenings of the world to Odin.

Odin also met a shape-shifting giant named Loki. Odin and Loki became blood brothers.

After many years on his journey, Odin learned of a witch named Mimir. She granted travelers a drink from her magical Well of Wisdom, but at a great price. Odin would agree to any sacrifice that would help his sons.

Odin dressed in a dark blue cloak and carried a walking stick to the well. But, Mimir recognized Odin! She knew Odin wanted the knowledge to cure his son's blindness.

Mimir tricked Odin into giving up one of his own eyes as his sacrifice. Then, she let him drink from the Well of Wisdom.

Odin happily did so thinking he'd be able to help his son. Instead, Odin gained knowledge of the past, the present, and the future.

As Odin drank, he saw all the sorrows and troubles that would fall upon men and the gods. Odin saw that his son would remain blind. He also saw that Loki had tricked Hoor into killing his brother Baldur.

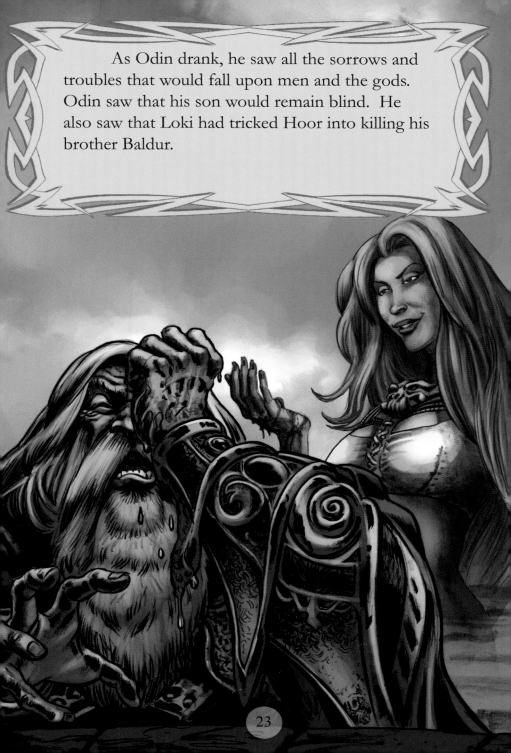

Mimir then tossed Odin's eye to the bottom of the Well of Wisdom. Odin was enraged. He cut off Mimir's head and returned with it to Asgard. There, Mimir was forever forced to foretell the future for Odin.

Odin spent many of his remaining years in the hall of Valaskjálf atop his throne. He was very wise, and he did his best to look after his kingdom.

Though it saddened him, Odin banished Loki from Asgard. Loki was determined to get revenge. So, he gathered the giants and other monsters into a great army.

27

Odin had seen the future in the Well of Wisdom. He knew what was to come. So when it was time, Odin prepared his kingdom for Loki's attack on Asgard.

The battle was called Ragnarok. It happened just as Odin had seen it in the Well of Wisdom.

Odin was swallowed by Loki's son, the wolf Fenrir. Loki was the last to die. In the end, the gods and their world were destroyed.

But, Odin knew the Norse people would always remember the gods. He also knew that as the flames of Ragnarok died out, a beautiful new world was born in its place.